FIONA MOODIE was brought up on an apple farm near Cape Town.
In 1972 she came to Europe, teaching English in Madrid and travelling
through the continent. She has lived in Italy, where she began to illustrate
children's books, and also in an isolated farmhouse in Provence, where she
spent much of her time painting. Fiona has illustrated many picture books,
including *Haddock* by Jan Mark, *The Wonder Shoes, The Boys and the Giants*
and *Nabulela*. Her latest title for Frances Lincoln is *Noko's Surprise Party*.
Fiona moved back to South Africa in 1991 where she lives in the Cape
with her psychiatrist husband and their twin daughters.

Mbombo hills

Takadu and Noko live here

flat rocks

big rocks

bathing pool

hippo creek

crocodile river

pangolin place

paperthorn tree

hyena caves

crocodile river

mud-bath

valley of 1000 anthills

For Anna and Clara - F.M.

Noko and the Night Monster copyright © Frances Lincoln Limited 2001
Text and illustrations copyright © Fiona Moodie 2001

First published in Great Britain in 2001 by
Frances Lincoln Children's Books, 4 Torriano Mews,
Torriano Avenue, London NW5 2RZ
www.franceslincoln.com

First published in the USA in 2001 by Marshall Cavendish

This edition published in Great Britain and the USA in 2008

British Library Cataloguing in Publication Data available on request

ISBN 978-1-84507-981-1

Printed in Singapore

1 3 5 7 9 8 6 4 2

Noko and the Night Monster

Fiona Moodie

F

FRANCES LINCOLN
CHILDREN'S BOOKS

Takadu the aardvark and Noko the porcupine were old friends. They lived in a little house at the foot of the Mbombo hills. They had to work hard for a living but there was always time for fun.

Every evening, Noko
cooked soup for
dinner. As he worked,
Takadu would sing
a song to make it
cook faster:

O, lovely pot, shu shu shu,
It's surely not, shu shu shu,
Too much to ask, shu shu shu,
To boil our soup, shu shu shu,
And do it fast, shu shu shu.

Noko's soup was
D E L I C I O U S !

But as soon as it got dark, Takadu said he was afraid of the Night Monster. Every bedtime it was the same. Takadu would shiver and shake, and Noko would read the wool prices from the *Farmer's Weekly* until he fell asleep.

In the morning Takadu always forgot how frightened he'd been the night before, and he would play his guitar, or talk to the dung beetles, or take the drum man for a walk. But Noko didn't forget. Noko was getting tired of reading the wool prices every night.

"What is this Night Monster anyway?" asked Noko, one morning. "Why don't you draw him for me so I'll know what he looks like?"

While Noko made clay pots, Takadu spent the morning trying to draw the Night Monster.

"That's him – that's the Night Monster," said Takadu at last.

And this is what he had drawn:

Next day, Noko got up early and crept out of the hut, taking Takadu's Night Monster picture with him. He left a message for Takadu:

Gone foraging.
Back this evening. Soup in pot.
Noko

First he went to see Mrs Warthog in her mud-bath.

He showed her Takadu's picture and explained what
he wanted to do. Mrs Warthog snorted with laughter.
"Of course I'll come," she said. "Mr Warthog can babysit
for a change. I'll see you when the moon is full!"

Noko found Pangolin at the river. He showed him
the picture and told him what he wanted him to do.

"Won't Takadu be upset, though?" asked Pangolin.
"Well," admitted Noko, "he might be at first.
But I think it'll be worth it in the end."
Pangolin smiled a shy, slow, Pangolin smile.
"All right then," he said. "I'll join you at full moon."

It was nearly dark when Noko came across Hyena.

Hyena shook with giggles when Noko showed him the picture.

"Hee hee hee!" he guffawed. "What a brilliant idea! You can count on me, Noko – I can't wait for full moon."

Stars had begun to shine in the evening sky by the time Noko got home. Takadu was very glad to see him.

"You've been away all day," he snuffled, "and the soup's cold and I've made up a new song but it's really, really sad."

"I'm sorry, Takadu," said Noko. "Why don't I make us some fresh, hot soup?"

As Noko cooked, Takadu sang his new song and he felt much better. Then they went off to bed, and Noko read the wool prices until Takadu fell sleep.

A week later it was the night of the full moon.
Noko said he had to go out and take his sick
cousin some medicine.

Takadu was very frightened. He would have to go to sleep without the wool prices, and what about the Night Monster?

All at once, Takadu heard Noko's voice calling from far away.
"Takadu, Takadu!" and then again, "Takadu! Takadu!"

"I'll have to find Noko," Takadu said to himself. "I'll take the
broom to beat the Night Monster, and I must find Noko."
Takadu shivered and shook, but he tiptoed out.

Where was Noko's voice coming from?
Takadu approached the rocks. They seemed even
bigger tonight. And what was that behind them?

It was the **Night Monster!**
Takadu didn't jump. He didn't scream. He shook
from his head to his toes, but he didn't run away.

Noko's voice came from behind the rock.

"Takadu! Takadu! Hurry up!"
Takadu charged right at the Night Monster and he
beat it **WHACK!** with the broom, right in its middle.

The most amazing thing happened.

The Night Monster came apart!
Takadu got such a fright that he fell on his back,
and Noko popped up, quite unharmed, from behind a rock.

Takadu was furious.
  "That was a really
HORRIBLE thing to do,
Noko," he snorted.
  "I thought you were in
danger. You made a
fool of me and now
I'm CROSS!"
  "But Takadu, you were
so brave!" said Noko.
"I called you and you
came to find me in the
dark! You whacked the
Night Monster! You
beat the Night
Monster! No more
Night Monster!
Takadu, you're BRAVE!"

Takadu started to laugh.

"All right, Noko, I forgive you. At least I'll never be afraid of the Night Monster again."

"Thanks, Takadu," said Noko. "And now, let's have a party!"

So all the animals went back to the
hut and ate lots of sweetcorn and
drank lots of marula berry juice,
and when the sun came up,
they were still singing and dancing.

Now the party has begun,
Let's jump and jive, we'll have some fun.
Night Monster is no more,
Takadu kicked him out the door.
We are the friends who dance and sing,
We're not afraid of ANYTHING!

Mbombo hills

Takadu and Noko live here

flat rocks

big rocks

bathing pool

hippo creek

crocodile river

pangolin place

paperthorn tree

hyena caves

crocodile river

mud-bath

valley of 1000 anthills

MORE TITLES FROM
FRANCES LINCOLN CHILDREN'S BOOKS

Noko's Surprise Party
Fiona Moodie

Takadu is planning a surprise birthday party for Noko and everyone is invited —
except greedy Hyena. Takadu works very hard to make Noko's birthday special,
but angry Hyena is trying to spoil the plans. Will he ruin the day or will the
two friends think of a way to make everyone happy…

ISBN 978-1-84507-587-3 (HB)

Snail's Legs
Damian Harvey
Illustrated by Korky Paul

"I am the King's chef," the man said, "and I am looking for an animal with
very strong legs to help me prepare a special birthday treat for him.
You are both such fast runners, you must have very strong legs indeed!"

ISBN 978-1-84507-642-9

The Cow on the Roof
Eric Maddern
Illustrated by Paul Hess

Every day Shon goes out to the fields to plough and sow and weed,
while his wife Sian works at home in the farmyard — until one day Shon starts
to feel he's doing all the hard work. "All right!" says Sian. "Tomorrow I'll go out
and do your work and you can stay at home and do mine."

ISBN 978-1-84507-591-0

Frances Lincoln titles are available from all good bookshops.
You can also buy books and find out more about your favourite titles,
authors and illustrators on our website: www.franceslincoln.com